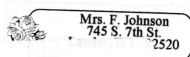

FRIENDS FOREVER

written by Carol Reinsma
pictures by Nathan Cori

STANDARD PUBLISHING
Cincinnati, Ohio

The Standard Publishing Company, Cincinnati, Ohio
A division of Standex International Corporation
© 1993 by The Standard Publishing Company
All rights reserved.
Printed in the United States of America.
00 99 98 97 96 95 94 93   5 4 3 2 1

ISBN 0-7847-0096-6
Cataloging-in-Publication data available

Edited by Diane Stortz
Designed by Coleen Davis

CONTENTS

FRIENDS HELP

Ant put pickles

in a basket.

She put in sandwiches.

"I want someone special

to come to my picnic,"

she said.

Bee knocked on the door.

"Is anybody home?"

yelled Bee.

The picnic dishes

rattled in the sink.

Ant did not answer.

"Bee is too noisy

to come to my picnic,"

said Ant.

"Ant, are you home?"

yelled Bee again.

Ant opened the window.

"Who is making

all that noise?" she shouted.

"Please go away!"

Ant closed the window.

She washed the picnic dishes.

Bee knocked again.

"Go away," said Ant.

"I am busy.

I cannot get ready

for my picnic

with all your noise."

Bee buzzed away.

Ant made lemonade.

Bee buzzed by the window.

"Is anybody home?" she shouted.

"No," answered Ant.

"It is me, Bee," called Bee.

"I am still not home," said Ant.

Bee was sad.

She buzzed away.

Everything was ready.

Ant took the basket outside.

She took the lemonade outside.

She put a tablecloth

on the grass.

"Who will come to my picnic?"

she wondered.

No one came.

Ant sipped her lemonade.

It was sour.

It made her lips pucker.

Bee buzzed by quietly.

"Do you want some honey

for your lemonade?"

she asked softly.

"That would be nice!"

said Ant.

"And please stay

for my picnic."

"A picnic!" said Bee.

"I like picnics."

Ant and Bee ate pickles

and sandwiches.

They drank lemonade.

They told jokes.

Bee laughed noisily.

"Oops," said Bee.

"I will be more quiet."

"Don't worry," said Ant.

"You are my friend.

You can make noise."

A person who gives to others will get richer.
Whoever helps others will himself be helped.
Proverbs 11:25

FRIEND, BE CAREFUL!

Ant and Bee went to the park.

Spider was at the park, too.

"Stay away from Spider,"

said Bee.

"She makes trouble."

But Spider had a game

that went, "Beep! Beep!"

Ant moved closer

when Bee was not looking.

"I like your game," said Ant.

"I have more at home,"

said Spider.

"Do you want to see them?"

Ant looked back.

She could not see Bee.

"OK," said Ant.

She followed Spider

as fast as she could.

But Spider ran faster.

"You are a slow poke,

Stick Legs,"

said Spider.

Inside Spider's house

were games that went *zap*

and *beep* and *bang*.

Spider showed Ant how to play.

"Push this button," said Spider.

"Then push this button."

Ant pushed the wrong buttons.

22

"Come on, Bug Eyes," said Spider.

"Do it right."

"I can't," said Ant.

"Get out, then," said Spider

with a spit.

On the way home,

Ant met Bee.

"Get out of my way, Buzzy,"

said Ant.

She gave Bee a shove.

Bee fell down.

"Why are you so mean?"

asked Bee.

"I don't know," said Ant.

"I know why you are so mean,"
said Bee. "You have been
at Spider's house."
"Yes," said Ant.
"Spider has a temper," said Bee.
"Let's go to my house.
We will have fun.
I will not call you names."
"But I might call you a name,"
said Ant.
"Forget the bad things
you learned from Spider," said Bee.
"I forgot," said Ant.

"The name I want

to call you is friend."

Don't make friends with someone
who easily gets angry.
Don't spend time with someone
who has a bad temper.
If you do, you may learn to be like him.
Proverbs 22:24, 25

FRIENDS AND PHONES

Ant picked up the phone

to call Bee.

Ant listened,

but no one said hello.

"Hello, hello," said Ant

into the phone.

There was no answer.

"Bee, if you can hear me,

come over," said Ant.

There was no answer.

Ant put the phone down.

She set out blocks

and made a castle.

"I want to make a tower,"

said Ant.

"But I need Bee to help."

Ant picked up the phone.

"Hello, hello," she called

into the phone.

Bee did not answer.

Ant put the phone down.

She tried to build a tower.

The tower fell down.

Ant shook her head.

She picked up the phone.

"Bee, I need you

to come over," said Ant.

There was no answer.

"If you were a good friend,"

shouted Ant,

"you would answer me!"

But no sounds came

from the phone.

Then Ant heard someone buzzing.

It was Bee coming up the walk.

Bee carried a big bag.

"I brought some blocks," said Bee.

"We can build a castle."

"Did you hear me on the phone?"
asked Ant.

"No," said Bee.

"But I called you," said Ant.

"Did you push the numbers
555-4383?" asked Bee.

"Oh, no!" said Ant.

"I did not push any numbers.
Next time I will remember
the numbers."

Bee and Ant laughed.

Bee looked at Ant's castle.

She looked at the tower that fell.

"It looks like I came

just in time," said Bee.

"Yes," said Ant.

"You are always here to help me."

A friend loves you all the time.
A brother is always there to help you.
Proverbs 17:17

UNDERSTANDING FRIENDS

Ant jumped rope.

"One foot, two feet,

three feet, four," she sang.

Cricket stopped to watch.

"That looks like fun," she said.

"Will you teach me?"

Ant showed Cricket how to jump.

They jumped until they were tired.

Ant opened a jar

of honey from Bee.

"Bee is a good friend,"

said Ant.

"But Bee told me

you are skinny and stinky,"

said Cricket.

She ate the last of the honey.

Ant walked back and forth.

"I guess Bee is not my friend

after all," she said.

Cricket skipped away

with Ant's jump rope.

Ant tried to read.

But she could only think

about Bee.

Ant made tea.

But without Bee's honey,

the tea was not sweet.

"I need to talk to Bee,"

said Ant.

Ant found Bee under the shade

of a yellow flower.

"Bee!" called Ant.

"I want to talk."

Bee flew away.

"No," she called back.

"You said I am sticky and fat."

"I did not," said Ant.

Bee landed on the yellow flower.

"Cricket told me so," she said.

"And Cricket told *me* you said

I am skinny and stinky," said Ant.

"You are my friend," said Bee.

"I would not call you names."

Ant and Bee found Cricket.

"You lied to us," said Ant.

Cricket put her head down.

"I did not mean it," she said.

Ant patted Bee's round tummy.

"Bee is not fat," said Ant.

"This is a honey tummy."

"And Ant is not stinky," said Bee.

"Her special smells

lead other ants to food."

"Friends like each other

for who they are," said Ant.

"You are right," said Cricket.

"How can I show you

I am sorry?"

"You can sing for us!" said Ant.

So in the glow

of the evening light,

Cricket chirped a sweet song.

Ant made tea.

And Bee put a drop

of honey in each cup.

A wise person is known for his understanding.
He wins people to his side with pleasant words.
Proverbs 16:21